DINNER
AT ALBERTA'S

DINNER
AT ALBERTA'S

by Russell Hoban

pictures by James Marshall

A Yearling Book

Published by
Dell Publishing Co., Inc.
1 Dag Hammarskjold Plaza
New York, New York 10017

Yearling ® TM 913705, Dell Publishing Co., Inc.

ISBN: 0-440-41864-X

Reprinted by arrangement with
Thomas Y. Crowell Publishers,
a division of Harper & Row, Publishers, Inc.

Printed in the United States of America

First Yearling printing—October 1980

CW

125211

DINNER
AT ALBERTA'S

"Arthur," said Mrs. Crocodile to her son
one evening at dinner, "you are eating
like a regular little beast."

"He won't close his mouth when he chews,"
said Arthur's sister, Emma,
"and I have to sit across from him,
so I have a good view of everything."

"Whuzzhuh maher?" said Arthur.

"Don't talk when your mouth is full,"
said Father. "Little bits of ravioli
are landing on your sister and no one
can understand what you are saying."

"It's awful," said Emma.

"It certainly is," said Mother.

"Everybody always picks on me,"
said Arthur when his mouth was empty.

"Look," said Emma,
"now he is feeling the saltshaker."

"Don't feel the saltshaker, Arthur,"
said Father. "Either take some salt
or leave it alone."

"My goodness," said Arthur,
"dinner around here is no fun
if everybody is going to pick on me,"
and he began to diddle with his spoon.

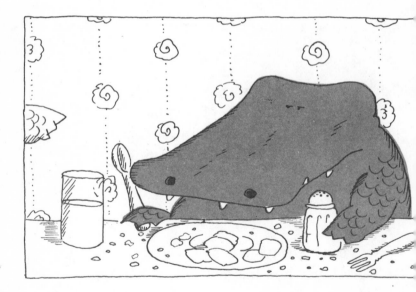

"Arthur is diddling with his spoon,"
said Emma.

"Emma," said Father, "you do not
have to report everything to me.
I am sitting right here
and I can see perfectly well."

"Arthur has no manners," said Emma.

"Why does everybody pester me so much?"
said Arthur. And he left the table
without excusing himself
and played his electric guitar
very loudly in his room.

"Between his table manners
and his electric guitar that boy
will destroy the world," said Mother.

"Maybe the world will get him first,"
said Emma, and she excused herself
and went to clean the tomato sauce
off her dress.

The next morning on the way
to the office Mr. Crocodile told
his friend John Hippopotamus about it.

"One way or another, boys are trouble,"
said John. "Take my sons, for instance.
They seem to think that just because
we live at the bottom of the river they
can track mud all over the living room."

"That's shocking," said Mr. Crocodile.

"It is," said John Hippopotamus,
"but my boys have beautiful
table manners, as far as that goes."

Then they both read their newspapers.

That evening at dinner
Arthur chewed with his mouth open,
felt the saltshaker,
and diddled with his spoon again.
He also knocked over the milk pitcher
while reaching for the beef stroganoff
instead of asking Father to pass it.
Then Arthur wiped up the milk
with a sponge, dropped the sponge
into the beef stroganoff, was sent
to finish his dinner in his room,
tripped over his music stand,
cleaned the beef stroganoff off the rug,
and played his electric guitar
very loudly, very late.

The next afternoon Mrs. Crocodile
went shopping with her friend Minnie Boa.
"What am I going to do with that boy?"
Mrs. Crocodile asked Minnie.

"It's hard to say," said Minnie.
"We eat only once every two weeks,
so it isn't too bad at our place.
But my children are terrible squeezers.
We haven't got a whole piece
of china or crockery in the house,
and nobody will play with them anymore.
Broken ribs all over town."

"I suppose we all have our troubles,"
said Mrs. Crocodile,
and both ladies bought new hats.

The next day after school
Emma brought home a friend,
Alberta Saurian.
Alberta was very pretty,
and when Arthur saw her
he brought out his guitar
and his amplifier and played
very fancy music very fast.

"This is my brother Arthur," said Emma
to Alberta.

"How do you do," said Alberta.

Arthur nodded and played faster.
They could not hear him above the noise
that came out of his amplifier,
but they saw his mouth say, "Hi."

"He's nice," said Alberta to Emma.

"He's very sincere," said Emma.

When Emma asked Mother if Alberta
could stay for dinner, Mrs. Crocodile
was not sure about it. "You know why,"
she said to Emma.

"I know," said Emma. "But people
are going to have to find out
about Arthur sooner or later.
We can't lock him up. Can we?"

"No," said Mother. "We can't."

"Then we'll just have to
take our chances," said Emma,
and she and Alberta set the table.

At dinner Arthur stared at Alberta
for a long time and did not eat.

"Arthur likes you," Emma whispered
to her friend.

"He's very shy and polite, isn't he?"
said Alberta.

"Eat something, Arthur," said Father.
"You haven't touched your food."

"I guess I'm not hungry," said Arthur,
and he picked at his cauliflower.
Arthur mostly ate bread and butter
and drank milk that Father
poured for him.

He watched to see how
Alberta took a little butter
from the butter dish and put it
on her plate; then he did the same.
When she broke off a piece of bread
and buttered it, he did it the way
she did, and he smiled at her.

After Alberta went home Father said,
"For once dinner was a pleasure.
Alberta should come here every night."

"Arthur would starve," said Mother.

"Everybody always pesters me,"
said Arthur, and he went to his room.
He had Oreo cookies and malted-milk balls
there, and he ate them all up.

The next day Arthur said to Emma,
"When is your friend what's-her-name
coming around again?"

"Who?" said Emma. "Alberta?"

"Yes," said Arthur, "Alberta."

"I don't know," said Emma. "Why?"

"No reason," said Arthur,
and he played his guitar.

"What are you playing?" said Emma.
"I never heard that one before."

"Just something I'm fooling around with,"
said Arthur. "Something I made up."
And he blushed.

"Oho," said Emma. And the next time
she saw Alberta she said,
"Arthur is making up a song for you."

"Arthur is really adorable,"
said Alberta.

"I never thought of him that way,"
said Emma.

"He really is," said Alberta,
"and I am going to ask my mother
if I can invite you and him
to dinner at our house tomorrow."

"We'll need a little time," said Emma.
"Could you make it next week?"

"All right," said Alberta. "Let's
make it next Tuesday."

When Emma went home she told Arthur.

"Oh boy," said Arthur,
and he turned up his amplifier.

At dinner that evening Arthur
partly closed his mouth when he chewed.

"All the way, Arthur," said Father.

Arthur closed his mouth all the way.

"Don't hunch over your food as if
you were crouching to spring," said Mother.
"It won't get away from you."

Arthur stopped hunching over.

"The fork, Arthur," said Emma. "Watch how I hold it. Don't make a fist like that."

Arthur watched how Emma held her fork.

"Howmaydays wegot?" he said to Emma.

"Not with your mouth full," said Emma. "We have five more days. Lots of time."

Every evening Arthur practiced eating the way Mother and Father and Emma did, and for every dinner Mother cooked different things for him to practice on. On Monday night she said, "I ought to have made a cheese fondue instead of flounder. If they have a fondue tomorrow he's going to be in trouble."

"Arthur," said Father, "don't ball up your napkin in your left hand like that."

"Too many things to think about," said Arthur. He was breathing hard.

"Relax," said Father. "Listen to how Emma breathes."

"Too much," said Arthur,
letting out his breath.
"What's the good of it all?"

"All right," said Father. "Forget it.
Just eat at Alberta's the way you eat
at home, and let it go at that."

Arthur breathed like Emma.

"That's it," said Father to Mother.
"This is a turning point."

On Tuesday afternoon Mother made Arthur
take a shower and put on clean clothes
after school.

"I took a shower Sunday night,"
said Arthur.
"What do I need a shower for?"

"Why did you make up a song for Alberta?"
said Mother. "You wanted
to be nice to her, right?"

"I guess so," said Arthur.

"So smell nice too," said Mother.

When Arthur and Emma were ready to go, they rowed over to Alberta's house.

Mrs. Saurian and Emma had met before, and Alberta introduced Arthur to her mother. "Mother," she said, "this is Arthur Crocodile."

"How do you do, Arthur," said Mrs. Saurian. "I've heard so much about you."

"How do you do, Mrs. Saurian," said Arthur.

Mrs. Saurian put out her hand and Arthur shook it. He had practiced that with Emma and his mother.

"This is my brother, Sidney," said Alberta.

"How do you do," said Arthur.

"Hi," said Sidney. They shook hands. Sidney got a better grip than Arthur and he squeezed hard.

Then Arthur was introduced to
Alberta's sister, Marilyn, and when
Alberta's father came home he was
introduced to him.

Then they all sat down at the table.
Mrs. Saurian had cooked flounder.

"Oh boy," said Arthur, "I know this one. . ."

". . . is going to be delicious,"
said Emma. "We both love flounder."

"I'm so glad," said Mrs. Saurian.
"We're all very fond of it too."

Arthur was careful not to spill anything.
When he wanted potatoes he said,
"Please pass the potatoes." He used
breath control and he did not hunch over.
He kept his mouth closed when he chewed,
kept his napkin in his lap, and used
his knife and fork the right way.
Arthur noticed that Sidney ate mostly
bread and butter and drank milk.

Sidney watched how Arthur took butter
from the butter dish and how
he buttered his bread, and he did it
the same way. Arthur smiled at Sidney,
and Sidney made words with his mouth
without saying them out loud.

"Never mind that, Sidney,"
said Mr. Saurian. "You just watch how
Arthur eats, and maybe you can learn
some manners."

When his father was not looking, Sidney
said to Arthur with his mouth
but not out loud, "I'll get you later."

"Any time," Arthur said back the same way

Arthur did everything right at dinner,
and he talked too, when his mouth
had nothing in it.

"I hear you made up a song,"
said Alberta.

"Yes," said Arthur.

"That's wonderful," said Mr. Saurian.
"That's a real gift, to be able to do that."

Sidney made more words with his mouth.

After dinner they went into the living room and Arthur plugged in his amplifier and his guitar.

"Tell us the name of your song, Arthur," said Mrs. Saurian.

"Well, it is not exactly a song because it does not have any words," said Arthur, "and it is called *Alberta*."

"Oh boy," said Sidney, and he let his head flop over and rolled his eyes.

"I think that is very sweet, Arthur," said Mrs. Saurian.

Alberta blushed.

Arthur played his song with a lot of tremolo. All the Saurians clapped and cheered, and Arthur bowed.

"That was very, very pretty," said Mr. Saurian. "Really lovely."

"Thank you," said Arthur, loosening his necktie a little. "That is why it is called *Alberta*."

"Oho!" said Mr. Saurian,
and Alberta blushed again.

"Well," said Emma, "I think we should
be going now."

"Stay a little longer,"
said Mrs. Saurian. "I'm so pleased that
Alberta has found such nice friends."

"Come on back to my room," said
Alberta to Emma.

"Come on outside," said Sidney to Arthur,
"and I'll show you my tree house."

"Fine," said Arthur.

When Arthur and Sidney came back
their clothes were mussed up and dirty,
and Sidney had a puffed-up lip.

"I bumped into a branch," said Sidney.

Mr. Saurian lifted his eyebrows
and nodded his head slowly at Arthur,
and Arthur smiled and nodded back.

Then it was time to go home.

Arthur and Emma said goodnight
and thanked the Saurians
for a very pleasant evening.
Arthur also thanked Sidney
for showing him the tree house.

"Well," said Emma as they rowed home,
"you see how nice it is
to be with people
when you learn some manners?"

"Yes," said Arthur, "and I think
the nicest part of manners is
teaching them to other people,
the way I did to Sidney."

"That's what keeps the whole thing going,"
said Emma.

"It sure does," said Arthur,
and he whistled *Alberta*
all the way home.

MS READ-a-thon —
a simple way to start youngsters reading

Boys and girls between 6 and 14 can join the MS READ-a-thon and help find a cure for Multiple Sclerosis by reading books. And they get two rewards — the enjoyment of reading, and the great feeling that comes from helping others.

Parents and educators: For complete information call your local MS chapter. Or mail the coupon below.

Kids can help, too!